Four Walls

Four Walls

By
Tyree M. Braden

E-BookTime, LLC
Montgomery, Alabama

Four Walls

Copyright © 2011 by Tyree M. Braden

All rights reserved. No part of this book may be reproduced or transmitted in any form or by any means, electronic or mechanical, including photocopying, recording, or by any information storage and retrieval system, without permission in writing from the copyright owner.

This is a work of fiction. Names, characters, places and incidents either are the product of the author's imagination or are used fictitiously, and any resemblance to any actual persons, living or dead, events, or locales is entirely coincidental.

ISBN: 978-1-60862-307-5

First Edition
Published June 2011
E-BookTime, LLC
6598 Pumpkin Road
Montgomery, AL 36108
www.e-booktime.com

Introduction

This story takes place in the small town of Meridian, Mississippi. Being from a small town has its good and bad qualities. It's good because everybody knows everybody, but it's bad because everybody knows everybody's business. But you will be surprised about what goes on in the comfort of these people's four walls.

We have Mary, the undercover drunk, and Mike, her husband, the best three-point shooter this side of the Mississippi. They have three kids; two girls and a boy.

Then we have James and Kasha. James is the loving husband; you know, the kind that loves his wife so much that he has to beat her, but smart enough not to hit her in the face because they sit in the front row in church every Sunday. They have two kids; one girl and one boy.

Then we have April and Tony. They are newlyweds, and you would expect everything to be good since they've only been married eight months.

They all come together because they are friends and work at a law firm together.

Chapter 1

"Good morning ladies," April said. "How was your weekend?"

"Girl, too short. I didn't get any sleep! I was too busy getting ready for this new case I have coming up," yawned Mary. "What did you do this weekend?"

"Nothing really," April replied. "Just cleaned up around the house. You know, Tony's still not working yet! I'm trying to pay all these bills on my own. I wish I had a man more like yours Kasha. He's smart, hardworking, a man of GOD, and plus, he has money. That's what kind of man I need."

Kasha looked over at her and smiled. She thinks to herself, *"If only you knew. You're right. He's all those things you named. But you forgot to mention that he's a woman-beater."*

Two hours later, a guy walked up to the front desk with some flowers and asked for Mary. "Mary. Delivery at the front desk," April called her.

"Um...yes, may I help you?" asked Mary.

"Yes, I have some flowers for you, and I need you to sign here," he replied, handing her a clipboard and pen.

Mary signed, and the guy handed her the flowers and left. "Now that's what I'm talking about. Flowers at work," April said.

Mary smiled. "When you have a man like mine, it's no telling what you may get sent to your job." As Mary walked off, she laughed and said to April, "He could buy you some flowers!"

Kasha said, "Girl, gifts aren't everything."

"Kasha, I know you're not talking. Your man just bought you a brand new car."

This was how their week went by, and before they knew it, it was Friday.

Mary leaves early every Friday to pick up her kids from school. "I'll see you ladies next week. And don't forget to lock up. Later," Mary said, walking out the door.

"Bye," they said in unison.

Chapter 2

Now, Mary does get the kids, but before she does, she stops at the liquor store and gets her 2&2 — that's two bottles of Paul Mason and two cups of ice. She likes making two drinks at the same time; you know, one cup for the right hand and one for the left hand.

They got to the house, and she headed straight to the kitchen to fix her drinks. The kids looked at each other like, "Here we go again with this." Mary's youngest daughter cried. "I hate when Mommy drinks."

Four Walls

Her son told his sister that everything was going to be okay. That's when her oldest daughter said, "Don't worry, Daddy will be home soon, and I'll ask him if we can spend the weekend at Granny's house. Just go into your rooms until he gets here."

About two hours later, Mike came home, and the kids rushed to the door. "Daddy, we missed you," they said in unison. The son asked, "How was your day at work?"

He hugged them and picked up the youngest. "It was good. How was school?"

They said that it was good. The oldest asked, "Dad, may we go over to Granny's house this weekend?"

"Why?"

They didn't say anything, and he realized that it was Friday. This was the day Mary gets drunk. "Yeah, just let me ask her."

On the other side of town, James and Kasha were having a family dinner, and everybody was having a good time, laughing and joking around, playing cards. Kasha thinks to herself, *"I wish he was like this all the time. Where did we go wrong? The laughing stopped and the beating started. I used to think I had the best life and the perfect husband, and two beautiful kids."*

"Baby, it's your turn," James said to Kasha. But Kasha was so deep in her thoughts that she didn't hear him. "Baby, baby," James said, waving his hand in front of her face. "Kasha, you hear me," James said, getting mad. He hits the table, causing Kasha to jump.

"Huh?" Kasha said.

"Are you going to play or not?"

She made a move and then leaned over and said, "Baby, I'm going to go check on the kids. Let somebody take my turn."

James was thinking, *"I know she didn't just get up from this table,"* but he said, "Okay. I'm going to go check on you in a minute."

She left and checked on the kids, then went into her room to watch TV. Then her phone began to ring. James heard it and yelled down the hall, "Yo, phone ringing!" She answered it and walked down the hall, talking to April about a case coming up.

The kids are downstairs watching TV. She started back towards her room and started laughing. James started getting mad, but was trying to keep his cool around their family and friends. He excused himself and headed to the room.

Overhearing her talking about Tony, he started to think, *"This girl is cheating on me! I'll kill her before I let her cheat on me."* So, he opened the door, looked at her, and then returned back down the hall, telling everybody that Kasha was on a business call. About two hours later, everybody started to leave.

James started cleaning up, and Kasha fell asleep. The kids are downstairs watching television. James walked down the hall and slammed the door, waking Kasha. "You must think I'm crazy."

Kasha sat up, startled. "What are you talking about?" she asked, looking over at him.

"I know you're cheating on me."

Four Walls

Kasha opened her mouth to reply, but James took off his belt and started to whip her like a little kid. She began to scream from all the pain. The kids heard the noise and ran up the stairs. They stood outside the door and James Jr. asked, "Why is Daddy always beating on Mommy?" His sister didn't answer him, so he said, "I'm going in there." He knocked on the door.

"Who is it?" James yelled.

"It's me, Little James. I heard Mommy crying. Is she okay? Daddy, open the door. I want to check on my mommy."

"Baby, I'm okay. Go back downstairs with your sister. Me and Daddy are just playing. I will be down there in a minute."

James looked at her and pointed to the bathroom. She went in there, washed her face, fixed her hair, and put on some sweat pants. When she got down the stairs, Megan looked at her and said, "So, is this how a lady is supposed to be treated?"

Kasha put her head down and said, "We were just playing."

Chapter 3

By this time, Tony was at the house waiting on April, and his phone rang. "What's up baby? How was work?" he asked, happy to hear from April since he hadn't heard from her all day.

"Long," she said with an attitude.

"Oh, are you on your way home?"

"Yeah. What's up?"

"Nothing. Just hungry. Trying to see what you wanted to eat."

"Something. I'm ready to eat and lie down."

"There's nothing else you need to do before you go to sleep? That's it?"

She sighed, "That's it."

"You sure?" he asked.

"Yeah, that's it." She knew where he was going with this. "Look Tony. I'm tired. You know today was supposed to be my off day. So, I'm really not in the mood for you and your games. I'm ready to eat, take a bath, and go to bed."

"You haven't been in the mood, and it's been two months, three weeks, four days, and six hours. We haven't had sex, and I've been patient, but what about me? What about what I want?" he asked.

By this time, April had become agitated. "Okay. You want to talk about what you want. What do you want, Tony?"

"Okay. I want more sex. I mean, damn. We've only been married for eight months. We should be having the best time of our lives. We should be humping like two wild monkeys."

"You done?"

"Yeah."

"Okay. Now, I want you to get a real job. I want you to start taking me out to dinner. I want you to buy me a card, some flowers, or some candy. I want you to get my hair done, get my feet done. Shit, buy me a piece of gum. That's what I want, Tony."

"Well, damn, April. That's how you really feel? It's cool. But let me tell you about the sorry man you got. I get up every morning and cook you breakfast. I keep this house clean. I keep your car clean, and yes, I do put gas in your car from time to time. When things break around here, who fixes it? Me. When your mother's car broke down, who fixed it? Me. I would love to do the things for you that you want, but it's really hard out there. I'm really trying to find a job."

"Yeah, I know. My phone is dying. I'll be home in a little while."

"Okay. Love you."

"Love you too," she said, hanging up.

As she was driving home, her low fuel light came on. She pulled up at a gas pump and went inside. "Can I get $10 on five?" She reached into her pocket, but couldn't find her money. She started to pat her back pocket and said, "I'm so sorry. I left my money in my truck."

The guy behind her overheard and reached around her and said, "Let me get $40 on five."

Four Walls

She turned around and said, "Wait. I'm pump five."

He smiled at her. "I know. I'm paying for your gas. And add this bag of chips for me." He looked back at her, "Do you need anything else out of here?"

She looked at him in much confusion. "No, I'm good. But thanks."

She walked back out to her truck. As she was standing there pumping her gas, she smiled to herself. He pulled up alongside of her and asked if that was enough gas. She smiled at him, "Yes, thanks again."

"No problem. You know it's not a good idea for you to be out here at night by yourself without any money, especially at this time of night."

"I know. I have $10 in my truck. You can have it, just wait." She reached into the truck but couldn't find it.

"Sorry, I don't have that either. My husband must have spent it."

He looked at her, "Wait a minute. You're married but riding around broke?"

She rolled her eyes, "Yeah, well, thanks again, but it's getting late, and I have to get home."

He smiled, "Okay, well, before you do, let me leave you with my business card. You never know when you may need help again."

She took it and read it aloud, "Braden, Braden, & Braden Law Firm." His name was on the back: Greg Braden embossed in gold lettering. She smiled.

All this was happening while Tony was at home scrambling his brain for something quick to eat. "Okay, let's see what we have here." He opened the fridge. "We have bread, cheese, and ham. I know my baby likes my grilled cheese. Plus, it's something quick."

As he was setting the grilled cheese on the table, April came in smiling. "What's up? Why are you smiling so big? You happy to see me?" he asked, smiling at her.

Her smile faded. "No. I was just thinking about something."

"Oh, okay. Sit down. I cooked dinner."

"What is it?"

He pulled a napkin off her plate. "It's grilled cheese," he said.

She looked at him. "Grilled cheese? Really? I've been at work all day, and the best you could come up with is grilled cheese," she said with disgust. "I'm not hungry." She walked off. "Grilled cheese, really?"

Tony just stood there, not knowing what to do. He started cleaning up, then sat down on the couch and turned on the TV. April took a shower and got in the bed, and the whole time Tony was just sitting there thinking. He cut the TV off and went to sleep right there on the couch.

He had a dream where he was talking to April. *"It's raining outside, and I'm missing you more and more. Sometimes I just look at your side of the bed, grabbing your pillow, wishing it was you I was holding, smelling, kissing, crying on, talking to; because when I close my eyes, it reminds me of you."*

Chapter 4

A couple of months pass by, and everything was still about the same with all four ladies; almost everything. April and Greg are starting to get closer, and it's around break time when Greg shows up to take April out for lunch. "What's up, little lady?" he said to April.

"Hey, Greg," she smiled.

"I was in the neighborhood and just stopped by to see if you were hungry."

"Yeah, just let me get my coat."

By the time she came back, Mary and Kasha walked around the corner. "Who is this, April?" Kasha asked.

April smiled, "This is my friend, Greg. We're about to go get lunch."

"This doesn't look like Tony to me," Kasha inquired, to see if Greg knew about Tony.

"He doesn't look like Tony to me either. He has money. Tony doesn't."

Mary joined in, "If he has a job, you need to keep him around."

April laughed. "Okay. I will see you guys when I get back," she said as she and Greg headed down the hall.

Once they were out of sight and earshot, Greg stopped to watch April walk. "Damn. That's all I have to say."

She stopped and turned to him, saying, "What?"

"I love to see you walk. It's like your ass has a mind of its own. It just moves by itself. Your ass reminds me of some spinner rims. Every time you stop walking, it's still moving."

"Boy, you are so crazy. I'm glad somebody likes it."

"You know, I wish I could give you my eye. That way, you can see what I see every time I look at you. How beautiful you are."

"That's so sweet, Greg. Thanks. I'm glad I met you."

"I'm glad we met too."

Meanwhile, back in the office, Mary and Kasha were sitting around talking. "Kasha, girl, you have a good man. I see the way he opens the door for you; always pumping your gas; keeps your car clean. Now that's a good man."

Kasha looked at her. "Your man does the same things for you."

"True that. He does."

Just then, James walked in. "What are you ladies talking about?"

Mary said, "About how good of a man you are."

James looked Kasha in the eyes. "Well, you know what they say. Behind every good man there's a good woman." Kasha smiled.

"Okay. I'll see y'all," smiled Mary. And with that, Mary left.

"You ready? I came to take you to lunch."

Mary walked back for her purse in just enough time to hear, "Go ahead. April should be on her way back, and plus, we're moving kind of slow."

Kasha thinks to herself, *"Damn, what now?"*

So, Mary went back to her office and called the flower company. "Hello. Yes, this is Mary Smith. I need a bouquet of flowers delivered to my job tomorrow around ten-thirty. Okay. And my address is on file with you all. Okay, thanks. Bye-bye."

While April was on her lunch break with Greg, Tony was still at the house and couldn't find any steady work. Sitting at the kitchen table thinking of something to do, a thought crossed his mind. *"Man, things have to get better for me and my girl. I don't have a lot of money right now, but here is my love letter to you."*

Dear 4 letter word,

I spend so much time talking to you that I feel like I know you so well. You're the reason for me being the

way that I am. I mean, sometimes I hate you, then I want you. Now, I miss you. Damn, now I'm lost without you. I think I'm going crazy for you. I'm sorry if I hurt you. Please come home. I need you. Can we talk? Okay, I won't do it again. Now, I'm crying for you, drinking because of you. Now, dreaming about you. I can't sleep without you. I need you, dear 4 letter word.

The phone rings and interrupts Tony's thoughts. "Hello."

"Hello, yes. This is MLGW. We are calling to let you know that you are past due on a bill of $145. This was due on the 1st of this month. When will you be coming in to pay it?"

"Next week, on Tuesday."

"Okay, let me make a note of this. I have you down for next week on

Tuesday. Thank you, sir. Have a nice day."

"You too."

As soon as he hung up, he heard a knock at the door. "Who is it?"

"It's me."

"Come in." Tony knew it couldn't be anybody other than his Uncle Charles.

"What's up, Tony?"

"Nothing much. Still looking for some work."

"Well, I could always use some help. I just got two new yards, Mr. Johnson's yard and Miss Braden's yard over on 2nd Ave."

"Okay. Let me call April and let her know what's up."

"Alright. I'm in the truck waiting."

"Okay, and thanks Unc."

He called April to share the good news, but she didn't answer, so he left a voice mail. "Baby, I was calling you to let you know that I'm about to go with Uncle Charles. He has a couple of yards he needs help with. Love you, and I'll be home later."

Meanwhile, April and Greg were sitting inside the car kissing. James and Kasha were walking to their car, and Kasha looked over at them. James told her to keep walking, so she looked ahead. James went on saying, "That's what's wrong with women now. They're always sticking their nose in other people's business."

"Get in the car," James told her.

"Okay," she said as she started to get into the front.

"What are you doing?"

"I'm getting in like you said."

"No, get in the back. And when you get in, go ahead and take them

Four Walls

panties off. I only have 15 minutes left on my break."

James got in the back and started putting it down. It got so good to him, that he closed his eyes and started asking whose it was. Kasha went along, saying, "It's yours, big daddy."

James' toes started popping and his legs began to shake. He screamed, "I'm coming! Don't move!"

"Okay." *I haven't moved yet. And it's been a whole minute.*

James smiled, "You sure you can go back to work after that?"

"I'm going to try," Kasha said, panting like something had really happened.

"Okay. Well, get cleaned up, and then get out. I'm running late. I have 13 minutes left on my break."

"A whole two minutes, and he wonders why I buy so many batteries," she said to herself.

"Okay."

They kiss, and she got out and headed into the building at the same time as April. "What were you thinking, kissing him?"

"Kasha, look, everybody doesn't have a man like James. Plus, it was just a kiss. That's not cheating. I still love Tony, and me and Greg are just friends."

"Yeah. Kissing friends. Remember April, never leave the one you love for the one you like, because the one you like will leave you for the one they love."

"Kasha, we are just friends."

"Okay. If you say so."

Four Walls

They got back into the building and were still talking about what happened outside. Mary joined them.

On the other side of town, Mike was pulling up to his mom's house to get her opinion about what's going on with his wife. "I'm just in time to help."

"Yes you are. I need you to wash my car. Those damn birds keep shitting on my car. They keep it up, and I'm going to shit on them."

Mike laughed. "Mom, you nasty."

"Shut up, boy. If R. Kelly can piss on people, then I can shit on birds."

"If you say so, but the kids want to know if they can come over here for the summer."

"Why? Is everything okay?"

"Not really. It's Mary. Her drinking is getting out of control. She does good Monday through Thursday, but

Friday… sometimes I hate to come home. Last week, it took me and one of the girls to pick her up off the floor."

"What happened, baby? Wait. Before you tell me, let's go into the house. I think them greens I ate are starting to come out on me."

"See, that's what you get talking about shitting on those birds. Now you are about to shit on yourself," Mike said, laughing.

Chapter 5

While his mom was in the bathroom, Mike walked around the house. He was looking at old pictures of him and Mary before the kids. Then he walked to his old room. *"I had some good times in here."*

His mom came out spraying. "Don't go in there for about 35 to 45 minutes," she said, laughing.

"Wash your hands, baby, and fix me something to drink."

"Okay."

"So, Mary got off work Friday. She beat me home. I took the kids out to eat. We got home about nine, and she was already drunk. I got out of the car and walked into the house. The kids went into their rooms, but I went to the living room. She was lying on the couch with one shoe on and one shoe off, a bottle in one hand, and a cup of ice in the other hand. You know, one thing about drunks, no matter how drunk they are, they will not drop their bottle. So, I got her up off the couch and tried to get her to the room to lay her down, and she told me to let her go. She said she could walk and that she didn't need my help. Then she hit me. So I asked her why she hit me, and she started talking about me and the kids don't love her, saying that only her bottle loved her. Then she said, 'Let's go to the room and do it right quick.' I told her no, and she was like, 'See, you

Four Walls

don't love me no more,' and started to cry. I told her I did and to stop crying. I told her that me and the kids did love her and not to cry. I told her that I wanted to make love to her, just not while the kids were up. She told me that if I loved her, to give her a kiss. I told her no again, because her breath smelled like hot dog water, and to show her I wasn't trying to hurt her feelings, I offered her a high-five. We high-fived, then I led her to the room, promising her that we would make love. But Mom, here's the craziness. I put her in the bed and went to the living room to clean up, and before I made it, I heard a big boom."

"What happened?"

"She tried to get up to go to the bathroom on her own and fell in the hallway. The kids came out to see what happened, and the boy said, 'There goes Mommy again.' The baby girl started to cry. I just told them to go back to their room. The oldest girl said that she would help me. So we picked her up, and she pissed all over herself. Mom, I'm tired, and the kids are sick of seeing her like that. It's the same thing every weekend. I can't take this no more. I'm ready to wash my hands of this mess."

"I guess you are pissed off or tired of getting pissed on."

"Mom."

"Okay, but I got one more. Let's hold hands. Would you please sing along if you know the words: Piss on me when you not strong. I'll be your friend that you can piss on. I'll wait for you, but don't take too long. R. Kelly got somebody for me to piss on, when you…"

"Mom, that's not funny."

"Yes it is. I think I just pissed my pants."

"Whatever, I'm gone."

"Okay. Okay, I'm done. Sit down son. Leaving Mary is not going to help the situation. She has a real problem, and you know that girl loves you."

"I know she does. It's just her drinking is becoming too much. But why is she drinking?"

"That's a good question, son. I think it has a lot to do with her job. Being a lawyer is a hard job, and if you think about it, before she took that big case, y'all were just fine. So, you need to find out what happened that day in the court room."

"I'll start there first."

"Then you need to start talking to her more. Ask her how her day is; take her some flowers to her job, because it seems to me that she's turning to the bottle for help, so you be her bottle. Okay?"

"Okay. I got to go. Love you."

"Love you too, baby. And yes, the kids can come over this summer."

"Thanks."

As Mike drove down the street, he thought to himself, *"What happened that day in court? I remember her saying that a young man got killed. He was sitting in his car when two guys walked up to him and robbed him. They took his money and then shot him. Damn, I'm going to surprise her tomorrow on her job and take her out to lunch."*

Chapter 6

While Mike was planning a surprise for Mary tomorrow at work, Mike's mom called and told the kids that they could come over for the summer.

Meanwhile, James was across town going through all of Kasha's stuff, smelling her panties and smelling her clothes. *"I know she's cheating on me with this Tony cat,"* he thought.

So, while James was digging through her stuff to see what Kasha was up to, Uncle Charles and Tony were on their way to Miss Braden's house over on 2nd Avenue to do some yard work. And during all of this, Kasha, April, and Mary were still talking about what happened earlier. But nobody was really thinking about the kids. And Kasha's daughter was getting real comfortable with her new boyfriend.

"Good morning ladies."

"Good morning. Why are you smiling so hard, April? You and Tony must've had a lot of fun last night."

"No. If you must know, Tony spent the night with his uncle. He's been helping him with some yard work, but Greg took me out to dinner last night," April said with a smile.

Kasha was confused. "Greg? As in 'he's just a friend' Greg?" asked Kasha.

"Yes, Kasha. Greg."

"You're young. Girl, you kill me. You have a good man at home that loves you."

"So what? If he can't find a good job, then it doesn't matter."

"I've seen that man cut grass, wash cars, and do anything else for a little taste of change. Yes, I know it's hard, but he tries. April, you married that man for better or for worse, richer or poor."

"I know, but I'm tired of living check to check. Shit, Greg has money, and he doesn't mind spending it on me."

"Mary, please tell her that there is nothing wrong with what I'm doing."

"There is nothing wrong with what she's doing," Mary said, not really listening.

"Thank you, Mary."

"You know what, both of y'all are wrong. See, you think you got time to play for both sides: Tony, the loving husband; the man who cooks and cleans for you; the one who loves your dirty drawers. Then we have Greg; the one with the nice car and all the money, but let me tell you about something called time. Time is one of the most important things in life. That's something you can never get back, no matter what. No matter how much money you have, how good you look, or who you know, you can never get back a lot of people's valuable time. Time is not like a cheap cell phone you can buy from Wal-Mart or the corner store. When my time runs out, I can't go buy more time. Time waits for no one. Value your time and value the time of others, because one day your time will run out."

"Thank you for Kasha's words of the day. Now, it's time for me to get to work."

So, they started their work for the day. A guy walked in 30 minutes later. It was Mary's weekly flowers. "Yes, I have a delivery for Mary."

"Okay. Let me buzz her. Mary, delivery at the front desk."

Mary came to the front as Mike was walking through the front door. They didn't notice each other until they got to the front desk. Mike was looking at Mary like, "What is this, and who is sending you flowers?" Mary was looking at him like, "What the hell are you doing here."

"Who sent you flowers?" She said nothing, so Mike took the card out of the flowers, and to his surprise, he saw that it was from Mike to Mary. "Who the hell is Mike?"

"Your name is Mike."

"Yes, I know. My name is Mike, but I didn't send you any flowers," Mike said, turning to the delivery guy. "Is this your first time delivering flowers here?"

"No sir. We come once a week."

"And they all come to her?"

"Yes sir."

"Okay. Thanks." He turned to Mary, "So, let me get this straight. You have another man sending you flowers to your job?"

"Mike, it's not what you think. Let's go into my office."

"Don't put your hands on me. Remember, you don't need my help, and I don't need this shit. For the past three years, I've been there when you were too drunk to go to work. I

Four Walls

was the one calling in for you when you were passed out on the bathroom floor, covered in your own throw-up. I was there. Or when your ass got so drunk, that you couldn't make it to the bathroom, I was the one cleaning up piss off the floor, and where was this Mike? If he can send you some flowers, he can help pay some of these bills. I'm waiting. You can't say nothing. You know what, don't even fix your mouth and try, because I don't care anymore. I'm gone," he said and left.

"Well, damn, Mary. Are you okay?"

"Yeah, I'm good."

"You want to talk about it?"

"No. Look, if anybody calls, tell them I'm gone for the day."

"Okay."

"I'm headed to my office to get my stuff," Mary said, heading down the hall.

The phone rang, and April answered, "Hello."

"Good morning. Put Mary on the phone, please. Tell her that it's Grandma."

"Okay. Let me page her." April put her on hold. "Mary, line one. She said to tell you it is Grandma."

"Okay. I got it. Hello."

"Hey baby. Are you okay?"

"Yes, I'm okay."

"I heard what happened. That boy called me crying, talking about he can't take it no more. He can't believe you're cheating on him. Baby, what's going on?"

"It's a huge misunderstanding, Grandma. I'm about to get off work.

I'm going to come over there. I can't really talk about this at work."

"Okay."

So, as Mary was getting her things and headed out the door, April and Kasha were talking. "Girl, I didn't know she drinks. I can't believe she is still pissing on herself."

"Damn! Look, that's our girl. We need to have her back on this."

"Okay. I'm going to go buy her some Pampers. I wonder what size she needs," April said, as if it was a joke.

"April!"

"What? I'm trying to help."

"You're acting as if your life is going good. You have no room to talk about anybody. You can't decide between your husband or your trick."

"Greg is not a trick, Kasha. You're just getting mad because you know you're the only one with a good man who has money."

"Having money doesn't make you a good man," Kasha said, more to herself. "So, that's your man now? You need help. You are going to find yourself by yourself."

"Whatever. I'm going to check on Mary."

April got up and headed down the hall. She got almost to Mary's office when she came out. "Look, you and Kasha take a couple of days off."

"Why?"

"Because I said so. We all got some personal matters we need to take care of. It's not just me. So I'm giving everybody time off with pay. So enjoy this," she said, heading to

Four Walls

the door. "Hey, Kasha. Can you lock up when everybody leaves?"

"Yeah. No problem."

"Okay, see y'all next week. Later."

"So, what do you have planned for the next couple of days?"

"Nothing, really. Clean up around the house. Nothing much, and let me guess, you're going to be spending time with your man, Greg."

"Yes."

"You know, Tony is a good man, and if you don't want him, just let him go. Do you know how many women are out there looking for a good man? You have one and act like he's nothing."

"Look, I never said that Tony isn't a good man. I'm just tired of being broke."

"Is money the only thing you think about?"

"No. I think about other stuff."

"Like what?"

"I think about sex too."

"Have you and Greg had sex yet?"

"Yes. And girl, it was good. He did some things to me that Tony would never do. Girl, he…"

"April, stop right there. Whatever Greg did is nothing new. If you like different things, tell Tony what you like. Show him how you want it, but talking to you is like talking to a wall, so I'm going back to work."

So, they went back to work. April called up Greg and let him know that she had gotten a couple of days off and checked to see if he wanted to hang out. He agreed, and they made plans to meet at Applebee's after work.

While they were on the phone, Kasha called the house and Megan answered. "Hello."

"Hey. What are you guys up to?"

"Nothing much. Dad and Little James are gone, and I'm just over here with my boyfriend watching a movie."

"Okay. Just make sure y'all stay in the front room."

"Okay."

Across town, Uncle Charles and Tony just finished cutting Mr. Johnson's yard and were heading across the street to Miss Braden's house. Tony knocked on the door, but nobody answered. "Okay, let's wait 10 minutes, and if she doesn't come back by then, we're going to just try again tomorrow."

About 20 minutes passed by, and nobody came home. "Okay. Let's go, Tony."

"Okay. Let me call April. I haven't heard from her all day."

He stepped to the side and called her. She didn't answer, so Uncle Charles just dropped him off at home.

Chapter 7

By this time, Mary was heading to her grandmother's house to tell her what happened earlier. She tried calling Mike again, but he didn't answer. She left him a voicemail saying, "We need to talk. This is all a big misunderstanding. Please call me back. I love you."

While she was leaving the voice mail, Mike just looked at the phone, pulled up into the driveway, and told the kids to get some things and that they were going over to their grandmother's house for a few days.

The oldest looked at him. "Is everything okay, Daddy?"

"Yes, just get your stuff ready."

Now, Mike and Mary are headed to grandma's house.

Kasha was headed home to make sure Megan wasn't doing anything with her boyfriend.

Uncle Charles dropped Tony off, and Tony headed to start cooking for April. He called her to see if she wanted some steak, but he still didn't get an answer. "Whatever. I'll just leave that there and clean up and take a bath. By the time I'm finished, she should be home, and she can tell me then."

So, three hours later, April came through the door, and Tony was sitting there with flowers, waiting on her. "Hey baby. Is everything okay?

I've been calling you for two days and haven't gotten an answer."

"Yes, Tony. Everything is okay. I've been busy with work, that's all."

"Okay. I took some steaks out to cook. I wasn't sure what you wanted to eat with them."

"Thanks baby, but I went out to eat after I got off work. You can fix yourself something, but I'm about to take a shower."

"Okay. I'll be waiting on you when you get out. I'll give you a nice rub down. If you want, I can come in there with you."

"Tony, is sex the only thing that you think about?"

"Yeah. We haven't had sex in three months. I'm tired of using my hand. I need some loving, and I know I've been working hard lately. I have to. Do you think I like working these part-time jobs? I have two strikes, and if I mess up one more time, I'm going away for a long time. On top of that, every time I fill out an application, they ask if you have a criminal history. If yes, you have to explain. I do, and by the time they read that I have a drug charge, they all say the same thing. 'We will call you and let you know something,'" he said, mimicking them. "So, I wait and wait, but they never call. So yeah, I think about sex. I need to feel some type of love. Shit, I'm running around here like I'm some kind of maid; going to the grocery store, putting gas in your car, cleaning the house up, cutting the grass, washing windows. Damn, I'm doing all of this, plus I get up every morning cooking breakfast and looking for a job. And you have the nerve to tell me that we can't have sex."

"Damn. I never looked at it like that. I'm sorry baby. Meet me in the bathroom in five minutes."

So, as they were taking their bath and making love, Tony was smiling from ear to ear. The whole time, it was getting so good to him that he started saying April's name.

Across town, Megan and her boyfriend made it downstairs to Megan's room. "You have a nice room."

"Thanks."

"So, what time are your folks coming home?"

"They should be here in a minute. Why do you ask?"

"I'm trying to see if I can get you out of those shorts before they get here."

"I don't think I'm ready for that yet."

"Why not? You know I love you, right?"

"You do?" she said with a smile.

"Yeah, I do. So can I get some?"

"Okay, but we have to hurry up."

As they were getting ready to do it she told him that it was her first time and to go slow and make sure he had a rubber on. He told her he had one on and that he would go slow.

About 10 minutes later, they heard a car pulling up. "Stop. Stop, it's my mom." So, they hurried up, got dressed, ran upstairs, and sat on the couch.

Kasha walked in. "Hello."

"Hey Momma."

"What y'all doing?"

"Nothing. He was just about to leave."

Four Walls

"Baby, when he leaves, take the trash out. It stinks in here. Y'all smell that? It smells like fish in here. Megan, you don't smell that?"

"No, ma'am. I don't smell it."

"Well, I do. Spray something in here. I'm about to take a bath."

Megan grabbed the trash and walked outside. Then she kissed her boyfriend and told him to call her later.

By this time, her dad was pulling up. "Where's your mom?"

"She's in the house taking a bath."

"Okay. Y'all stay out here and play."

"Okay."

So, James walked in the house and smelled sex. "Kasha! Where are you?"

"I'm in here taking a bath. How was your day at work?"

"Why does my house smell like sex?"

"I don't know. I just got home. I asked Megan, and she said she didn't smell anything."

"I bet that little hot ass girl was having sex in my house. Wait till she gets home. I'm gonna whoop her ass."

"Wait, James. I'll talk to her myself. Don't put your hands on my baby."

"Okay. You know what? It was you. That's why you ran into the house and took a bath; to get the smell off of you in a hurry. Now get your ass out of the water."

As soon as she stepped out of the water, he started beating her with a wet towel. Megan and Lil' James came in the house and hear her crying. Megan walked into the bathroom. "Momma, why do you let him constantly beat on you?"

"Because I love him."

"So, if they love you, it's okay for them to beat on you?"

"No, baby."

Lil' James handed her some tissue. "Here Momma. It's going to be okay. Stop crying. The next time he puts his hands on you, I'm going to shoot him."

"Lil' James, don't talk like that. He is still your daddy. I'm okay. Lil' James, take your bath. Megan, reheat that food and tell your daddy his food is ready."

So, Megan walked downstairs and said, "Daddy, do you love Momma?"

"Yeah, I love your momma. Why do you ask me that?"

"Why do you beat on her?"

"You're too young to understand."

"Whatever. Your food is ready."
James went upstairs to eat.
Meanwhile, April and Tony were lying in bed together, cuddling. April got a text from Greg.

Greg: "What's up lady? I'm over here thinking about you."

April: "What are you thinking about?"

Greg: "I wish we never did it, and I wish I never loved it. Girl, now I'm so deep in love with you that there's no way we can just be friends."

April: "You got me smiling, and Tony is lying right here. I'll text you later."

Four Walls

"Who was that baby?"

"Oh. That was Kasha from work."

"Okay." Tony got up and reached into his pants pocket. "Here. It's not much, but it's just something to help you out on the bills."

"What time do you have to be at work?"

"About eight, but I'm gonna leave here about seven because we got some more yards."

"Okay." They lay back down.

Over on the west side, Mike and Mary were pulling up at his mother's house. Mike jumped out of the car. "Ma, what is she doing here?"

The kids started asking him why she was crying, thinking that she was drunk again. Mary told them that she wasn't. She asked Grandma to take the kids into the house so that she could talk to Mike. As soon as the door closed, Mary started talking. "Mike, before you say something, listen. I'm not cheating on you. I've been sending flowers to myself every week. Baby, I'm sorry. I should have told you."

"Yes, you should've."

"Mike, do you think you could ever forgive me?"

"I don't think I can. You've put me and the kids through a lot." He looked at her. "Can I ask you something?"

"What?"

"In the court room three years ago...."

"Mike, please, I don't want to talk about it."

"But I do. Ever since that day, you've been drinking hard every Friday."

"I know. And I'm sorry. That's the only thing I can do to help me sleep. I can still hear his momma screaming, 'Not my baby! He didn't do it!' We had a case we were working on, and Miss Jones' son was charged with armed robbery. He was only 17. He was a good kid; never got in trouble before. He was a 3.0 student. His cousin picked him up from school. To make a long story short, he robbed Super Stop. He led the police on a high-speed chase, and when the police caught them, they were charged with robbery. I tried and tried to win that case, but they gave that baby 10 years. His momma blamed me for him getting locked up. Two months later, I got a phone call. They found him dead in his cell. I felt so bad that I just started drinking to take the pain away."

"Baby, I'm sorry, but that was not your fault. You did all you could to win that case."

About this time, Grandma came outside. "Is everything okay?"

"Yes, we're trying to work it out."

"Baby, pray about it, and GOD will work it out."

Across town, Kasha, James, and the kids were having dinner. "Mom, may I be excused?"

James looked over at her. "Why?"

"Because I'm not hungry anymore."

"Sure, and take your brother with you," Kasha said.

They left the table, and Kasha looked at James. "James, I can't take this anymore. No matter what I do, it's still not enough. What happened to you? You used to be fun, now I hate to come home sometimes."

"Whatever. I'm going to bed. Clean up this mess," James said as he got up from the table.

Kasha started cleaning up, but as she cleaned, she thinks and starts to get mad. When she finished, she went downstairs, got Lil' James, and went into Megan's room. "I want y'all to get a few things and pack them into two small bags. We're going to a hotel tonight around 12:00 a.m., after your dad is asleep."

She kissed them, walked back upstairs, and laid down. Two hours later, she got up like she was going to the bathroom, went downstairs, got the kids, put her wedding ring on the kitchen table, and left.

James woke up at six as usual, but he didn't feel Kasha beside him.

"Kasha?" She doesn't answer. He gets up and goes downstairs, only to find Kasha and the kids gone. He went into the kitchen to see if she left a note. All he found was her wedding ring on the kitchen table. He looked around, angry, thinking, *"It's not over till I say it's over."*

Chapter 8

James gets up to go out looking for Kasha and the kids. Tony gets up to fix breakfast before he leaves. Mike and Mary spend the night at Grandma's house.

About 6:45 a.m., Uncle Charles is outside blowing the horn for Tony to come out. He kissed April. "I'm gone, baby. I love you." And with that, he was off to do Miss Braden's yard.

Kasha dropped the kids off at school, and since she was off, she was going to go look for a place for them to stay.

As Kasha was riding around, April was being awaked by her phone ringing. "Hello," she said, half asleep.

"Good morning, beautiful. Are you ready for today? I want to take you to meet somebody," Greg greets.

"Okay. Just let me park my car at work, and you can get me from there," April said, as she got up to get dressed.

"Okay, I'll meet you there in five minutes."

April got dressed and meets with Greg. "You look great," Greg said, stepping back to admire her. She blushed, and with that, they headed toward his mother's house, but what she doesn't know is that Tony and Uncle Charles were headed there too.

Greg and April get there and were walking around the house. Greg told a story for every picture. By this time, Uncle Charles and Tony had arrived and started on the backyard. Greg and April were still in the house having a good ole time.

Tony finished the back yard and was heading to start on the front while Uncle Charles cleaned up. At the same time, April and Greg were coming out the front door, laughing and kissing. Tony stopped and stared at her. "April, you know him?"

April turned around. "Tony? What are you doing here?"

"I'm here doing some yard work, remember? The question is, what the fuck are you doing here when you told me that you were going to work?"

Greg looked at April. "Baby, you know him?"

"Yeah man, she knows me. I'm her husband, but who are you?"

"I'm her boyfriend."

By this time, Uncle Charles came around the corner. "What's going on?" He follows Tony's gaze. "Well, damn. Now, Tony, I know you're mad, but don't start nothing."

"You better listen to him. You already lost your girl. Don't get your ass whooped too."

Uncle Charles turned to Tony. "Look, don't be mad at him. Be mad at her. Let me tell you something son." He turned to Greg. "If she left him because his money ran out, she would do the same to you."

Tony turned to April. "I just have one question. Why?"

"Because I'm tired of being broke, living check to check. I'm sorry Tony, but I need a man who can take care of me."

Uncle Charles grabbed Tony. "Come on Tony. You don't need a gold digger. She's going to get what's coming to her." They left.

Greg looked at April. "Baby, are you okay?"

"Yeah. Can we leave?"

"Yeah."

Chapter 9

Three months later, things seem to be better for these ladies. Mary slows down on her drinking. Kasha finds a new place. April moves in with Greg. Mike is spending more time with his kids and is helping and talking more to Mary. James is still trying to get Kasha back. Tony is crying and refusing to go to work with Uncle Charles. He calls April, but she hangs up every time. Or if he texts her, she doesn't reply. He feels as if he is lost and has nobody to talk to, so he turns to drinking and writing.

The Body

Girl, I'm missing your body, want your body, can I kiss your body, hold your body, caress your body, can I put my tongue on your body, all over your body, from your head to the bottom of your feet, making love to your body, sweat dropping off your body, long stroking your body, cum coming from your body now in the tub, bathing that body, got soap on that body, making love to your body, baby I love your body, want your body, miss your body, damn, I am in love with your body.

The Perfect Storm

You know if I was your man, my bad I am your man, you know sometimes I forget we are together, I mean sometimes I get up an hour early, just to watch you sleep, I start crying, sometimes I look up at the sky and thank the Lord for sending you to me, I'm sorry for calling your job so much, I just want to hear the sound of your voice, baby I'll have your dinner cooked, I'll rub your feet, just hurry home, I miss you, just come in and take your shoes off, your water is already ran, how was work, I'm down on one knee, baby please, please will you marry me, it hurts me every time you walk out of that door and you don't have my last name, baby me and you are the perfect storm, you can't have the rain without the

Four Walls

thunder and lightning, sun without the moon, night without day, and you can't have me without you.

The phone rang. Tony was too depressed to answer, so he let it go to voicemail. "Yes, I'm trying to reach Tony. This is Mr. Davis from the temp service. We found you a full-time job. Please call me…"

Tony rushed and picked up the phone. "Thank you." He set up an interview with them for Monday. As soon as he got off the phone, he went to the bathroom and freshened up. Then he was out the door heading to the barber shop.

On his way, he stopped at the corner store to get some skittles and ran into Kasha. "Hey, Tony."

"What's up, Kasha?"

"I heard what happened. I'm sorry that girl did you like that."

"Me too. But I'm okay. If you see her, can you give these to her?" He handed her the letters.

"I sure will."

By this time, James had finally caught up with her and came into the store. "So, this is the reason you can't answer my calls?" He turned to Tony. "And you must be Tony?"

"Yeah, my name is Tony."

He turned to Kasha. "Look, I got somewhere to go. Please make sure you give those to her."

"You ain't going nowhere," James said, pulling a gun out.

"James, put that gun down."

Before she could say anything, Tony hit James, and they got into a fight. Tony got the best of James and started to walk off. James took this chance to his advantage and picked the gun up. Kasha started to say something, but James told her to shut up before he shot her. Tony tried to run while they were talking, but James turned and shot Tony twice in the back. Kasha screamed, "No! That's April's husband, Tony! Somebody call the police!"

The ambulance showed up 15 minutes later. "What happened?"

"He got shot twice in the back."

"Okay, let's get him to the hospital. He's already lost a lot of blood. Hurry. Stay with me son."

Kasha tried to call April over and over again, but she didn't answer. She tried calling from Tony's phone. Still no answer, so she called Mary and told her what had happened. "I've been trying to call her, but she isn't answering. Call her and tell her to meet me at the hospital. Hurry."

Mary hung up with Kasha, called April, and told her what had happened. April rushed to the hospital. Kasha was sitting there in the waiting room. "I've been calling you all day. Knowing you, you were probably so busy laying up with that nigga that you can't answer the phone, while your husband is in there fighting for his life. I need some air. I'm stepping outside. Can you at least stay here until I get back?"

"You can go ahead and leave. I'm going to stay here with him."

"Well here. He told me to give you these. I would drop them, but you might not pick them up," Kasha said, handing her the letters.

April started reading, and the more she read, she began to cry. A doctor

Four Walls

walked by and noticed her. "Are you okay? You don't look so good."

April passed out. When she woke up, the doctor told her that she was pregnant. She just lay there. Finally, she spoke. "May I see my husband?"

"Yes, he is in room 227."

April got up, walked down the hall, and knocked on Tony's door. The nurse told her to come in. When she walked in, she saw a lot of tubes in Tony and broke down crying.

"It's going to be okay. The doctor was able to remove both bullets from his back," the nurse said to April.

"Will he be able to walk again?"

"I don't know. It's up to him, but I can tell you that he is a fighter. He kept saying that he's been through too much these last couple of months, and that he was not going to give up now."

As the nurse went back to doing her job, Tony woke up. "April, is that you?"

"Yes, Tony. It's me."

"What happened, baby?"

"You got shot. Don't talk too much. Just rest. I'm going to stay up here with you."

"What about Greg?"

"Someone once told me never leave the one you love for the one you like, because the one you like will leave you for the one they love. I was with Greg, but I'm still in love with you," she said as she reached into her pocket and pulled out the note that Kasha had given her. It had her wedding ring in it. She put it on. "I married you for richer or for poorer, better or for worse. Shot or not, we're going to get through this together, one step at a time."

From Tony to April

The Get Away Drive:

It's morning, and I'm getting ready for work. Damn, I got to drop her off at work again because her car is in the shop. "Baby, go warm up the car. Here I come." She sits in it while it's warming up, and as soon as I walk out the door, I realize that I've left my phone. I run back in, but before I get all the way in, I hear my car pull off and head down the street. I hear her scream, and I run to my garage. Not only has someone stolen my car, but they have my girl too. I jump on my motorcycle and rush down the street behind them. I'm thinking to myself, *"This nigga best not put his hands on my baby."*

The Sky

Just sitting here looking at the stars. I close my eyes for a minute and say to myself, "If I had one wish, I would wish that I could slow down time. That way we could spend more time together. When I look at the sky, I think of you, hoping you see the same things that I do. I wonder if you see the same stars as me. I'm looking at a shooting star, and I think of how far our love has to travel to reach one another. If I was from Mars and you were from Venus, every time I see a shooting star, I would hope that it's headed in your direction to bring you some of my love. When I look up at the sky, I know that nothing can keep us apart. Not the sun, the moon, the heavens, or the stars. I love you."